Boffin and Bat

Diane Wilmer

Illustrated by Alan Snow

Series editor **Penni Cotton**
Senior Lecturer, Reading and Language Studies
Kingston Polytechnic

To Parents

By sharing books together at home you can play a vital part in helping your child learn to read.

The books at Level 3 in this series are for children who are progressing towards reading fluently on their own. The play format gives the support necessary for children to enjoy reading with you and yet lets them read their own part and thus gain confidence as independent readers.

How to read this book together

▷ Make reading together a comfortable and special time.

▷ **The role of Bat is for you to read and your child reads Boffin**. Explain that you don't read out the speaker's name each time, it is just there to help tell you when it's your turn.

▷ Introduce the story slowly by looking at page 5 and talking about the characters. Perhaps your child is already familiar with them from other books in the *Parent and Child Programme*.

Help your child, particularly on the first reading, by giving the difficult words so you don't slow up the pace of the story or by reading both parts initially.

Encourage your child to use the pictures to guess or predict what is happening.

If your child is stuck just give the word yourself. This is far more helpful than sounding out individual letters.

Always praise good guesses — much of the skill in reading is in guessing or predicting what the word will be.

Your child will probably enjoy reading the story with you again and again — this is valuable in building confidence and practising reading.

Always end reading together on a positive note.

Bat   Hello, Boffin, is that your new computer?

Boffin   Yes, Bat, it's my new computer.

Bat   Can we play with it, Boffin, or go somewhere with it?

Boffin   We can go somewhere with it, Bat.

5

Bat   Can we go somewhere now?

Boffin   Where, Bat?

Bat   The seaside or the zoo . . . ? You choose.

Boffin   I like the zoo, Bat.

Bat   I love the zoo. Please take me to the zoo, Boffin.

Boffin   OK, Bat, let's go to the zoo.

Bat   Are you sure you've done everything properly, Boffin? I want to go to the zoo, not the moon!

Boffin   Silly Bat. I've done it properly. Off we go . . . wheeee!

Bat   Boffin, this isn't the zoo.
I can't see any animals.
You've made a mistake and
brought us to the wrong place.

Boffin   Ooh, Bat! I have made
a mistake. This isn't
the zoo.

Bat   Ugh! It's very spooky here.
I don't like it, Boffin. Let's go.

Boffin No, Bat. I like spooky places. Let's stay.

Bat NO! I'm scared. Look at my teeth, they're chattering. I'm shivering all over.

Boffin I'm not scared. Come on, follow me, Bat Baby.

Bat   Oh dear, Boffin. It's too quiet and empty in here for me. Come on. Let's go.

Boffin No, Bat. I like quiet, empty places. Let's stay.

10

Bat   Boffin! Boffin! Did you hear that loud bang?

Boffin   Yes, Bat. What was it?

11

Bat   There's a monster after us.
Ugh! A great big monster
with red eyes and sharp
pointed teeth that likes little
bats for tea!

Boffin   Silly, silly Bat, it was
the door banging.
Come on, follow me.

Bat   Eek! Did you hear that creak?
          I'm sure it's a monster, or a
          creepy ghost following us.
          I'm going, Boffin.

13

Boffin   It's not a monster and
it's not a ghost.

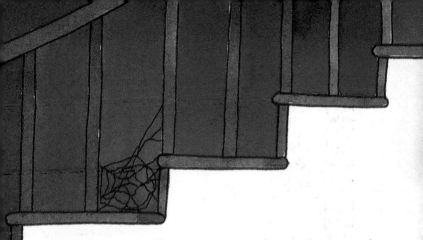

Bat   Well, it's something big and heavy and it's creeping up behind us.

Boffin   I'm big and heavy, Bat. It's me.

1 ... creak.

2 ... creak.

3 ... creak.

Come on, Bat. Follow me.

Bat   Eek! Boffin, I'm not coming up there. I don't like this nasty, spooky house. It's full of bashes and crashes and squeaks and creaks. I'm scared.

Boffin   Silly Bat! It must be mice.

Bat   I can't see any mice. Are they in the cupboard or under the carpet?

Boffin   They're here, Bat, in the cupboard.

Bat   Hello, little squeakers. You gave me a BIG fright.

17

Bat   Eek, Boffin, I can hear more spooky noises.

Boffin   What noises, Bat?

Bat   A horrible drip-drop, plip-plop. It might be a monster dripping blood.

Boffin   Silly Bat. It isn't a monster and it isn't blood. Look in here.

Bat   No! There'll be blood dripping from the tap.

Boffin   It's water dripping, Bat.

Bat   Ah! It's wet water too! My bat wings are soaked and soggy!

Bat Help me Boffin! Something's got me. It's squeezing me tight and smothering my face.

Boffin Oh, silly little Bat. It's a spider's web.

Bat   Get it off me, Boffin. I hate creepy, crawly spiders.

Boffin   Poor little spider.

Bat   Poor little ME! It's a whopping big spider and I'm frightened of it.

Boffin   No, it's frightened of you!

Bat   Boffin, did you hear that?

Boffin   What's the matter now, Bat?

Bat   A noise. A flap, flap noise, like a ghost shuffling up behind us. I think it's behind the curtains.

Boffin	It's not a ghost, Bat. It's the curtains flapping.
Bat	Phew! It sounded just like a ghost to me.
Boffin	Well, it isn't.
Bat	Oh no, Boffin. What's that?
Boffin	Come on, Bat. Follow me.

tip

tap

Bat   There's something out there, Boffin, it's that monster again. Listen to it, tapping and scratching on the window. Go away, smelly monster!

Boffin   Bat, it's not a monster.

Bat   Yes, it is and it's in that tree in the garden.

Boffin   No Bat! It's not a monster. It's the tree tapping against the window. Come on, follow me.

Bat　Boffin, look over there.

Boffin　I'm looking.

Bat　There's a lorry and lots of people.

Boffin　What are they doing?

Bat　I think they're moving in.

Boffin What, moving into this spooky house?

Bat Yes, Boffin, let's go. Set the computer and do it properly this time.

Boffin OK, Bat. It's set.

Bat Let's go to the zoo, Boffin.

Boffin Off we go . . . wheeee!

Bat   Here we are, the zoo at last.

Boffin   Phew! At last.

Bat   Let's look at the lions and tigers first. Then the rhinos. We must see the snakes and the fish too.

Boffin   The lions, tigers, rhinos, snakes, fish and the big bats too, Bat!

Bat Oh, Boffin, I'm so tired.
Can you take me home?

Boffin Yes, I'll take you home.
Off we go . . . wheeee!

eek! eek!

Bat   What a good day we've had.

Boffin   Yes, the zoo was good.

Bat   Shall I tell you a secret, Boffin?

Boffin   Yes, Bat.

Bat   I liked the house best of all.
It was really SPOOKY.

Boffin   Silly, silly Bat!

30